You Are a Famous Explorer Stranded on a Desert Island . . .

You are being pursued by your enemies. You jump into a ravine and arrange the bushes so that they will cover you. And then you wait. Just as your pursuers are upon you, you glance down. Two feet away from you is a huge snake. Your heart is pounding. Out of the corner of your eye, you see the snake rise from its coiled position. At the back of its neck a huge hood opens, and you know that this is a member of the cobra family, one of the most deadly species of snakes in the world. You want to scream in fear.

If you think you can stay until the pursuers pass, turn to page 135.

If you think the cobra is ready to strike, and you want to get out of there, turn to page 136.

TAKE YOUR FATE IN YOUR OWN HANDS BUT . . . TAKE HEED!

WHICH WAY BOOKS for you to enjoy

Available from ARCHWAY paperbacks

WHICH WAY BOOKS #4

FAMOUS AND RICH

R.G. Austin

Illustrated by
Mike Eagle

AN ARCHWAY PAPERBACK
Published by POCKET BOOKS • NEW YORK

AN ARCHWAY PAPERBACK *Original*

An Archway Paperback published by
POCKET BOOKS, a Simon & Schuster division of
GULF & WESTERN CORPORATION
1230 Avenue of the Americas, New York, N.Y. 10020

ISBN: 0-671-43920-0

First Archway Paperback printing March, 1982

10 9 8 7 6 5 4 3 2

Printed in the U.S.A.

IL 3+

FOR DANIELLE

Attention!

Which Way Books must be read in a special way. DO NOT READ THE PAGES IN ORDER. If you do, the story will make no sense at all. Instead, follow the directions at the bottom of each page until you come to an ending. Only then should you return to the beginning and start over again, making different choices this time.

There are many possibilities for exciting adventures. Some of the endings are good; some of the endings are bad. If you meet a terrible fate, you can reverse it in your next story by making new choices.

Remember: Follow the directions carefully and have fun!

Someone new is moving next door to you. You watch as the men unload all sorts of interesting objects from the van and carry them into the house.

After the van leaves, you walk over to meet your new neighbor. He is sitting alone on the porch, moving slowly back and forth on an old-fashioned porch swing.

You immediately like the old man's face. He has a long, gray beard, deep blue eyes and a voice that is strong, yet soothing and kind.

You talk for a long time—about life and dreams and distant places. As you sit next to him on the swing, you feel yourself becoming hypnotized by his gentle voice. You are about to drift off when you suddenly become aware that he has asked you an important question.

"Pardon me," you say. "I'm sorry, I didn't hear you."

"Your dream . . ." the man says. "What is your dream for the future?"

"That's easy," you answer. "I want to be famous and rich."

(continued on page 2)

"Ah," says the man. "Famous and rich are not what they seem."

"Why?" you ask.

"Because for everything you earn, there is a price; for everything you achieve, there are dues you must pay."

"But surely the result makes it all worthwhile," you say. You have always imagined that being famous and rich would be the most wonderful thing in the world.

"Sometimes it is worth everything. Sometimes it is worth nothing. Always remember: Happiness does not come with riches, nor contentment with fame."

"Well," you say, "I'd sure like to have a chance to find out."

"Do you truly mean what you say?" he asks.

"I most certainly do," you answer.

"Then you shall have that chance," the man says.

(continued on page 3)

Very slowly, the old man turns his back to you. You hear him mumbling strange sounds, and you see him moving his hands in weird circular motions. His body quivers; his head shakes.

Finally, he turns to you and asks, "Do you want to be an explorer, a movie star or a detective?"

If your answer is explorer, turn to page 4.

If you want to be a detective, turn to page 6.

If you want to be a movie star, turn to page 7.

You are in the pilot's seat of a twin-engine propeller plane. There is a copy of *Time* magazine on the floor. You are amazed to discover that your picture is on the cover. The headline reads: "Famous Explorer Sets Out for Mysterious Island."

You are flying low over the South Pacific, searching for a remote and uncharted island that you have reason to believe exists in this area.

You spot a mountain on the horizon and are sure that this is the island for which you have been searching.

Suddenly the plane sputters, and you are horrified to see flames burst from the engine.

You know that you have no choice. You must grab what you can and bail out.

Turn to page 9.

Suddenly, you find yourself sitting in a carved, antique chair behind an enormous desk. There are rows of electronic buttons on the desk. They open windows, close curtains, turn on TVs, dim the lights, raise and lower your chair. You are obviously a very wealthy detective.

The phone rings and you answer it.

"Please hold for a gentleman from the Federal Bureau of Investigation," says the operator. Soon, a deep male voice begins to talk. After explaining that he prefers to keep his identity a secret, the man gets down to business.

"I'm calling you because you are the smartest and the most famous detective in the world, and we of the FBI would like you to help us solve a serious problem."

"What is it?" you ask.

"I cannot tell you over the phone. If you want to accept the job, you must come to Washington immediately. Go to the FBI building and ask for Agent 337."

If you go to Washington, turn to page 11.

If you refuse the job because of other commitments, turn to page 12.

You are sitting in the back of the longest limousine you have ever seen. The seat is covered with an incredibly soft leather, and in front of you is a bar, a television set, a snack table and a telephone.

A uniformed chauffeur is driving you to the studio where you have an appointment with the producer of your next movie.

The limousine pulls to a stop near a crowd of people, and you climb out. A shriek of joy and excitement fills the air, and suddenly you are surrounded by the pushing, shoving, screaming crowd.

(continued on page 8)

"May I have your autograph?" says one voice. "Please sign this," says another. Others are grabbing at you, touching you, pulling on your clothes. One person is trying to pull a button off your jacket.

You rush back into the limousine for safety.

Turn to page 14.

You grab your emergency kit, which includes a self-inflating rubber raft, some rations and medical supplies. Then you open the cockpit and jump.

As you pull the rip cord on your parachute, you can see the island in the distance. You estimate that it is at least twenty-five miles away.

As soon as you hit the water, you disconnect your parachute and pull the cord that inflates the raft. Then you climb in.

(continued on page 10)

You look around and see that your parachute is still floating on the water.

If you try to retrieve your parachute, turn to page 15.

If you take the tiny paddle that is secured in the raft and immediately try to direct yourself toward the island, turn to page 16.

When you ask for Agent 337, you are led down a long corridor and into a small room. There is a loudspeaker on one wall.

"Welcome," says 337 through the speaker. "I hope you will be able to help us. You are probably not aware that our country is being flooded with counterfeit money. The bills are being printed in ones, tens and fifties. We have been working on this case for two months and have not been able to locate the counterfeiter. We need your help.

Turn to page 17.

You thank the FBI agent but explain that you have just returned from a long journey and have other obligations. Then you turn to your work.

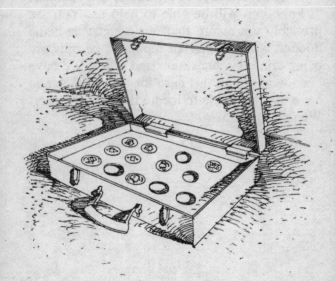

(continued on page 13)

A friend of yours is a rare-coin dealer. He has told you that one of his employees is stealing from him. Both coins and money are missing. He has asked you if you would try to find out who the culprit is.

As a favor to an old friend, you accepted the assignment.

If you think the first thing you should do is talk to an undercover informer with whom you keep in contact, turn to page 18.

If you go directly to the rare-coin store, turn to page 20.

The people press their faces against the one-way glass, and you are grateful that they cannot see inside.

"Take me to the back entrance, Charles," you tell your chauffeur. "Maybe I can sneak in there without anybody seeing me."

The chauffeur nods and drives away.

Relieved, you sink back into the seat and flip on the television before pouring yourself a soda.

Soon you realize that you are driving away from the back entrance. Then you notice that the fringe of hair showing under the chauffeur's cap is not black like Charles'. It is blond.

If you wait until the car slows down before trying to jump out, turn to page 21.

If you confront the strange man who is impersonating Charles, turn to page 22.

The sun beats down mercilessly on you as you struggle to grab the chute before it sinks.

Finally, you manage to hook your paddle around one of the parachute lines. You pull the heavy, soggy parachute aboard the raft and stretch it out so that it will dry in the sun.

By now, you have lost sight of the island. You are seized with a sudden feeling of panic. If you go in the wrong direction, you know that you could sail for months without finding land.

You are pretty certain that the island was on the western horizon when you saw it from the plane. But it is midday now, and the sun is directly overhead.

If you are quite sure that west is to your right and you would like to start paddling immediately in that direction, turn to page 16.

You think that perhaps you should wait for the sun to move so that you can deter-mine accurate directions. But you are worried that if you waste time, you will be forced to spend the night in the raft. If you choose to wait, turn to page 23.

You paddle for many hours and are exhausted when, finally, you see the island on the horizon.

Later, as you near the island, you discover that there is a mammoth bed of seaweed between you and the beach. It seems to go on forever.

If you fear that you might get tangled in the seaweed and would prefer looking for another approach to the island, turn to page 24.

If you want to take a chance by paddling through the seaweed, turn to page 25.

"We do have one clue," 337 continues. "We have just received word that yesterday a child in the Midwest received a stuffed pig in the mail. It turned out that the pig was stuffed with counterfeit money. Sending the child that animal may turn out to be the counterfeiter's first big mistake.

"Before you investigate the pig," says 337, "you may want to look at the lab report on the bills."

If you decide to visit the lab, turn to page 26.

If you want to go immediately to visit the child, turn to page 28.

You find Finke, the informer, in the old, decrepit hotel where he lives. You ask him if he has heard any underworld gossip about rare coins.

Finke nods. There is a faint smile on his face. But he says nothing.

"OK," you say, handing him twenty dollars.

(continued on page 19)

Finke nods again and says, "Word's out on the street that Jimmy the Fence has some rare currency to sell to somebody who is interested in Greek coins. But The Fence made it clear that the buyer had better be rich. And he also said that he wants to be paid in cash. I hear he's getting some new coins tonight."

If you leave immediately to find Jimmy the Fence, turn to page 29.

If you first go home to disguise yourself, turn to page 30.

Knowing that you cannot go anywhere without the risk of being recognized, you slip on a disguise before visiting the store.

Once inside, you see that there are three employees. You approach the first one and purchase a coin for $3.70. You give the salesperson the exact change.

You check the cash register, noting that the last amount rung up before your purchase was $12.85.

If you wait to see if the salesperson will ring up your sale on the cash register, even though you require no change, turn to page 31.

If you thank the salesperson and walk out of the store, turn to page 32.

You pretend to be absorbed in the television program, but actually you are waiting for the right moment to escape.

You know that the driver will have to slow down for the turn ahead, but you are also certain that he will turn with as much speed as possible.

If you decide to escape when he turns the corner, even though you will risk hurting yourself, turn to page 33.

If you would rather wait until the car must stop, turn to page 34.

"Who are you?" you ask.

The chauffeur says nothing. Instead, he pushes a button that makes the glass partition roll up, separating the front and back seats. Then you hear a click and see that he has locked all the doors.

You watch the countryside whiz past, and you realize that you must be traveling at least ninety miles an hour.

If you think you might be able to make a call from the car telephone that is to your right, turn to page 36.

If you look around for a weapon, turn to page 37.

You wait. You are already thirsty, and you can feel your skin burning in the hot sun. You spread out the parachute and, exhausted, you climb underneath it for protection.

If you decide to take a nap while you wait, turn to page 38.

If you think that you should stay alert and be on the lookout for danger, turn to page 40.

You start to paddle around the seaweed. It seems endless. After more than an hour, you finally round a corner of the island and see a clear path to the beach. You paddle toward shore.

Suddenly you hear strange, loud, barking noises. You look to your right just in time to see a family of sea lions dive into the water and

head toward your raft. You are uncertain whether it would be safer to stay in the raft or to jump out and swim for shore.

If you stay in the raft, turn to page 41.

If you jump out and swim for shore, turn to page 42.

You paddle into the seaweed and are amazed at how easily your raft slips through it. Soon you reach the shore and pull the raft onto the beach.

You are securing the raft on dry land when you feel a rope slip around you.

Stunned, you turn around to face a man and a woman.

"Who are you?" you ask.

"It is we who ask the questions," says the man. "Say nothing more until we take you to Mark, the leader of our group."

Turn to page 43.

You enter the lab and talk to the scientist who is working on the project. He gives you a detailed report. Then you inspect a one-dollar bill. The colors are a perfect match. The engraving is the exquisite work of a master. Even the paper has tiny red and blue threads in it, just like the real thing.

Then you take a magnifying glass and inspect the eagle. The eagle is holding a sheaf of fourteen arrows in one claw and an olive branch with fourteen leaves in the other. Over its head is a cluster of fourteen stars.

(continued on page 27)

Suddenly you remember that there should be thirteen arrows, thirteen leaves and thirteen stars, all representing the original colonies of the United States.

You know that the number fourteen must be some kind of clue.

If you think that the number fourteen may represent the state where the bills are being printed, turn to page 47.

If you think that the number fourteen might represent a person's initials, turn to page 48.

It takes most of the day for you to travel to the small town where the child lives. The journey requires two planes and a rental car. When you arrive early that evening, the mother and child are waiting for you.

After discussing the situation with the child, you ask if she has the wrapper in which the pig was mailed.

"It's somewhere in my room," the girl tells you.

"Well," you say with a smile, "then it shouldn't be difficult for you to find."

If you ask to see the pig, turn to page 49.

If you go to the child's room immediately, turn to page 50.

You locate Jimmy the Fence at his usual hangout—a disreputable bar. Taking care that he does not see you, you wait and watch for several hours.

Finally, a man comes into the bar. You recognize him as one of the employees in the rare-coin store. He is wearing a gray hat pulled low over his face, and a navy-blue windbreaker.

You watch as he talks to The Fence. Then they exchange something. You tail the employee out of the bar.

Turn to page 53.

You return home, disguise your face and dress in your best clothes so that you will appear to be a person wealthy enough to purchase the coins.

You decide that you would rather catch the thief in the store before he visits The Fence.

You walk into the store and strike up a conversation with the three employees. You admire an ancient Greek coin but say that you would rather have one embellished with the head of Alexander the Great.

You know that your friend has one of those coins locked in his vault, and that the employees know the combination to the safe. You tell the three employees that you are willing to pay sixty thousand dollars for the coin, which is half the price your friend wants to sell it for.

Turn to page 54.

You pretend to browse in the store while you watch the employee. He does not ring up the sale and you are certain that he intends to pocket the money; the longer you stay, the more certain you become.

Finally, the salesperson rings up your sale and puts the money into the register.

It certainly took him a long time, you think to yourself. He probably became suspicious of me.

You blew it. Now you will have to start all over again. Next time you will be more careful.

The End

You are afraid that the salesperson will become suspicious if you linger in the store, so you thank him and leave.

At the end of the day, after all the employees have gone, you return to the store and inspect the cash register tape.

Your suspicions are confirmed. There is no record of a sale for $3.70. You find the $12.85, but your purchase is not registered after it.

Since the salesperson did not have to open the cash register to give you change, no sale was recorded. He just kept the money.

"It is most likely," you tell your friend, "that every exact-change purchase goes into the salesperson's pocket—and not into the register."

"Brilliant!" says your friend. "I suspected him all along, but I did not want to prejudice the case by telling you ahead of time. You have produced the proof I need to catch the thief. No wonder they call you the best detective in the world!"

The End

The driver slows down, and you grip the door handle as the car moves into the turn.

Halfway around the corner, you open the door. You do not try to land on your feet; instead, you bend down and roll onto the pavement.

You hear the brakes of the car screech to a halt. You get up and start to run. When you discover that you are near a school, you run into the playground and try to hide yourself in a crowd of children.

Turn to page 55.

You wait for the car to stop, but you cannot believe your bad luck: All the traffic lights are green. Finally, there is a red light and the chauffeur is forced to stop the car.

As soon as he stops, you open the door, jump out of the car and start to run, knowing that the chauffeur cannot follow you in all this traffic.

You run across the street and call the police from a phone booth. You give them the license number and they assure you that they will pursue the kidnapper.

Relieved, you call a taxi and go home. You cannot stop thinking about your harrowing experience, and you are grateful that you have been invited to a party that evening at the Showoff mansion. You shower and change into your dressy clothes.

(continued on page 35)

When you arrive at the Showoff mansion, you notice that it is guarded by huge iron gates with a bronze dollar sign worked into the intricate design.

If you go straight to the pool behind the garden, turn to page 56.

If you go inside the mansion first, turn to page 58.

You look at the phone, but you are certain the chauffeur will see you in his rearview mirror if you put the receiver next to your ear. And so, very carefully, you lift up the receiver and place it in your lap.

You tap the receiver of the phone with your ring: ...---... Then you pause. ...---... You continue to repeat the SOS signal.

You know that the operator who transfers calls to the normal telephone lines will hear the signal; and soon, help will arrive.

The End

You take a bottle of soda out of the bar and grip it by the neck, ready to attack as soon as the car door opens.

Finally, the car turns onto a road between two cornfields and heads toward a farmhouse. You pass the old house and drive into the nearby barn.

Two men approach the car. They are wearing stockings over their faces.

If you decide that there is no way you can defeat three men with a bottle of soda, turn to page 59.

If you think that this might be your last chance to fight your way out, turn to page 60.

Thinking that you will take a short nap, you close your eyes. But you are so exhausted from tension and fear that you fall into a deep sleep.

Hours pass. When you awaken, it is dark out. The sky looks like a black velvet dome that has been lit up by trillions of silver spangles. It is the most magnificent sight you have ever seen. But in the midst of this beauty, you feel more alone than you have ever felt before.

(continued on page 39)

You look up and try to find the North Star so that you can get your bearings. Then you remember that it cannot be seen south of the equator. You are confused for a minute, until you find the Southern Cross, the four important navigational stars in the southern hemisphere.

From your studies in lifeboat navigation techniques, you know that if you face the Southern Cross, you will be looking south.

You know that the island lies to the west. You face the Cross.

If you direct the raft to the left, turn to page 61.

If you direct the raft to the right, turn to page 62.

You are exhausted and you fight to stay awake. You frequently reach into the ocean to splash your face with the cool water.

After a very long time, your head begins to hurt; then you hear a strange humming noise. You suspect that you are hallucinating; but when you peek out from under the parachute, you see a speck in the sky. When the speck grows larger, you realize that it is a search plane flying in your direction.

You wave the parachute frantically as the plane approaches.

Soon, the plane is flying over your head. It circles once and dips its wings, signaling to you.

You know it won't be long now before you are rescued.

The End

Suddenly, your raft is surrounded by at least forty sea lions. You are afraid that they will flip the raft over and you will be caught among them. Slowly, you continue to paddle toward shore. But instead of attacking you, the sea lions cavort playfully around your raft.

Comfortable now with the sea lions, you step onto the shore. Suddenly you hear a fearful racket, and then you see a mammoth bull sea lion heading toward you in a vengeful rage. You suspect that you have inadvertently invaded his territory.

If you decide to back off carefully into the water, turn to page 63.

If you run as fast as you can along the beach, away from the sea lion, turn to page 64.

You jump into the water and find yourself surrounded by baby sea lions. But instead of harming you, they want to play. You cannot believe it.

All around you they frolic, bringing you into their special world. A baby swims toward you and, just as he reaches your body, he dives under the water. You can feel his whiskers tickle your legs as he passes beneath you.

Happily, you swim with your playful escorts to the shore.

As soon as you are standing on dry land, you are horrified to see an enormous bull sea lion heading toward you, making a fearful racket. You realize that you have invaded the animal's territory.

Turn to page 63.

You stand before Mark. He is dressed like all the others—in articles of clothing that have been woven from palm fronds.

"Why have you taken me prisoner?" you ask.

"In our situation it is necessary," says Mark. "Many years ago, thirty people were shipwrecked and found a haven on this island," he explains. "For months, we spent every waking hour in constant efforts to find a way off the island. We built signal fires ready to be lit at the first sign of a plane or ship. We made SOS messages out of black volcanic rocks set in the white, sandy beaches. We did everything in our collective powers to be rescued.

"Gradually, about half of the group came to the conclusion that they liked it here.

"Here, there is no pollution. The air is sweet and clear, and the birds are our music. The stars at night are miraculously bright, for there are neither cities with lights nor layers of smog to wipe out the beauty of the night sky. The noises here are the noises of nature, and the scenery has not been tampered with by the poor taste and bad judgment of modern society. Our lives are sweet and simple and clean. We have no crime, and we have no overcrowded housing.

(continued on page 44)

"The only dangers to our lives are the wild animals that our ship was transporting to a zoo in the United States. But we have learned to live with them.

"One day I suggested that we stop seeking rescue, that we make our peace with our surroundings, and that we create a new—and kinder—life for ourselves and for our families.

"The group that agreed with me began to destroy the signal fires of those who wanted to be rescued. We removed the SOS signs from the beaches and scattered the rocks back where they came from.

"And now, sadly, we have split into two groups, each so opposed to the other that we constantly battle. We do not kill one another, but my group is pledged to sabotage any efforts that are aimed at rescue. We must ask that you abide by our rules here if we are to allow you to remain free."

(continued on page 45)

"But why don't you let the others be rescued?" you ask. "*You* would not have to leave the island. You could stay behind."

"Because once we are discovered, even if we remain, civilization would not be far behind. Soon our island would be turned into a resort. People would see how beautiful this paradise is, and they could not resist it. We would awaken one day and see concrete-and-glass condominiums dominating our beach. Our way of life would be destroyed.

(continued on page 46)

"You must make a decision now," Mark continues. "You will remain free if you agree with our ideas. Otherwise, you will be our prisoner."

If you think about your family and friends and cannot imagine giving them up forever, turn to page 65.

If you think you could live this tranquil life for the remainder of your days, turn to page 67.

Since the original pictures represent the thirteen colonies, you surmise that the counterfeit pictures represent the fourteenth state to enter the union. You check your almanac and find that the fourteenth state is Vermont. You head directly for Montpelier, the state capital.

You spend an entire week inspecting one engraving plant after another. On the eighth day, you see the headline of the local paper: MASTER COUNTERFEITER CAPTURED BY FBI.

Can't win 'em all, you say to yourself, angrily throwing the paper on the floor.

The End

You can see that these bills were created by a brilliant engraver. And you also know that there are few artists in the world who do not want to sign their names on the work they produce. No person likes to remain anonymous.

Since the initials work out to N.N.N., the fourteenth letter of the alphabet, you contact the engravers' union and ask to see a list of all the members.

You go directly to the Ns and find the name Norris Nathan Nutley.

You locate his address easily. Then you contact Agent 337 and give him the information. That same afternoon, he calls to tell you that the FBI has arrested the counterfeiter.

"I don't know how you did it," 337 says with admiration.

"Simple deduction," you reply.

"You're a genius," says 337. "A famous and rich genius."

The End

You look at the pig, inspecting it carefully. Other than the fact that this is the ugliest pig you have ever seen, you find nothing unusual—except for the stuffing.

"I think we should search your room now," you say.

"I don't think that's going to be as easy as you think," says the girl, with a smile.

"Don't be silly," you reply. "It's only a room."

(continued on page 50)

You follow the child up a narrow staircase. She tells you that her room is in the attic, and that her father fixed it up for her.

When she opens the door, you are staggered, appalled and shocked. The room is enormous, and it seems to you that every toy and game ever manufactured is scattered on the floor. There are Legos, Lincoln Logs, Barbie dolls, Ken dolls, a buggy, blocks, trucks, planes, hundreds of stuffed animals, a harmonica, pieces of string, a broken kite, a scattered Monopoly set, a baseball glove, a toy stove, a bikini, three sneakers, crayons, socks and paper. And those are only the things you notice at first glance.

(continued on page 52)

Everywhere you look there is a horrible mess.

"Now you know why my dad made the room in the attic," the child says. "Mom says that when I learn to keep this tidy, I can move back downstairs."

If you think that the girl might have thrown the wrapper in the closet, and you decide to look there first, turn to page 68.

If you want to start at the end of the room nearest the door and work your way across to the other side, turn to page 69.

You follow the man down the street and into a crowded arcade. You lose sight of him for a minute, and then you spot him at the rear of the arcade. You hurry through the crowd and catch sight of him just as he leaves through an emergency exit.

You tail the man to an apartment building, noting the address before you approach him.

When you put your hand on his shoulder, he turns around. You are astounded to discover that he is not the man you thought you were tailing. You have fallen for one of the oldest tricks in the business: The guilty man entered the arcade and hid, while a cohort, dressed exactly like him, led you away from the real crook.

Even the best detectives lose their men sometimes, you think ruefully—*and their money, too.*

The End

You ask the three employees to call you if they can locate the coin you have described to them. Then you go home and wait.

At ten o'clock that night, the call comes. The anonymous caller tells you that he has a Greek coin with Alexander the Great on it, and that he will sell it to you for sixty thousand dollars.

You agree to meet the caller in a dark alley. Although there is very little light, you think that you recognize him as one of the employees. But he is wearing a navy-blue windbreaker and a hat pulled down over his face. It is difficult to identify him for certain.

He hands you the coin and you examine it with a penlight. It is the coin you have requested. You give him the money.

If you tail the man, turn to page 53.

If you decide to go home and figure out a different strategy, turn to page 70.

You hope the chauffeur will not see you in the midst of all the children.

But suddenly a child screams out your name. Then all the children begin to shriek with excitement. They have never been so close to someone so famous.

You look over their heads and you see the strange chauffeur—staring at you through the fence.

If you decide to stay with the children and go inside the school with them, turn to page 71.

If you think you can get the children to help you, turn to page 72.

The back garden is as large as a football field. There is a swimming pool in the shape of a dollar sign, and everywhere roses are in bloom.

On one side of the garden is a silk tent, where an orchestra is playing rock music. At the end of the tent is a banquet table laden with an enormous variety of food.

(continued on page 57)

All around you there are people dressed in elegant clothes. There are more famous faces at the party than there are unknown ones.

If you feel like swimming and dive into the pool, turn to page 75.

If you are hungry and walk over to the banquet table to get something to eat, turn to page 76.

As soon as you enter the house, a butler takes your coat and leads you into the dining room. It is crowded with people wearing fancy clothes and jewels. The lavish display of food is incredible. You have never before seen such a feast. Anything you could possibly want to eat is on the table. The plates are rimmed in gold to match the chandelier, and the forks are also gold, with dollar signs engraved into them.

Just as you are about to take a bite of lobster mousse, you hear a voice behind you say in a loud voice, "Don't move. This is a holdup."

Turn to page 77.

The men open the door, and you step out of the limousine.

"This way, please," says one of the men, with a sarcastic sweep of his arm.

You look around. You see a rifle hanging on a nearby wall. And there is a horse tied to a post at the end of the barn.

If you try to lunge for the rifle, turn to page 78.

If you think you might be able to make it to the horse, turn to page 79.

You grip the bottle by the neck, ready to attack the men as soon as they open the door. You hear a click and realize that the chauffeur has released the locks.

When the stocking-faced men open the door, you spring toward them.

Turn to page 80.

You guide your raft to the left and set out on your journey.

You paddle all night, carried along by a swift current. You know that by morning you will have covered a great distance.

In the morning, you are facing the rising sun. It takes you a moment to realize that you have paddled in the wrong direction. You are alone and adrift in a seemingly endless sea.

The End

You start to paddle, making slow but steady strokes. You continue for what seems like hours, but you have no idea how much time has really passed.

You hear a low, ominous roar. The sound frightens you. As the roar grows louder, you realize that it is the sound of waves crashing on the shore.

Suddenly you feel the swell of a giant wave forming beneath your raft. You are thrown from the boat, but you are still clinging to the raft by a rope.

If you let go of the rope, hoping the wave will carry you to the shore, turn to page 82.

If you twist the rope around your wrist so that you do not lose the raft, turn to page 83.

You back into the water, knowing that the bull sea lion did not come for you until you stepped onto the dry land. *The beach must mark the beginning of his territory,* you think.

As soon as you are in the water, the bull stops his attack stance, and you know you are safe.

You take one more step backward and feel a searing pain in the calf of your right leg. You see a red stain in the water and know that you must have cut yourself on a sharp piece of coral.

If you try to swim out to your raft to get the medical kit, turn to page 84.

If you choose to swim along the shore until you reach a section of beach that is not protected by a bull sea lion, turn to page 85.

You run down the beach in a panic, the bull in pursuit. When you pass a large lava rock, the sea lion stops. You know that you have crossed the imaginary border of the bull's territory.

You stand on the sand for a moment and are suddenly aware that you are sinking, and sinking fast!

If you struggle to grab hold of a rock that is just out of your reach, turn to page 87.

If you flatten yourself out on the squishy quicksand, turn to page 88.

The thought of remaining a prisoner is repugnant to you.

Deciding that you have very little choice, you break away from the group of people and start to run. Logic tells you that the opposing group is probably living on the other side of the island.

There is only one problem: This is a volcanic island, and its center is made of a huge mountain.

(continued on page 66)

As you run, you can hear the men and women of Mark's group close behind you.

If you choose to climb directly over the top of the mountain, turn to page 89.

If you think you can make better time by going around the base of the volcano, turn to page 90.

"I will remain," you say. "This is, indeed, a beautiful way to live."

"Welcome," says Mark with a smile. "Now we must ask a favor of you. One of our people is very sick. Karen, the leader of the other group, is a doctor. But she trusts none of us. Will you go to her and convince her that we really do need her help?"

You agree to go and soon you are escorted close to the opposing camp.

Waving a white handkerchief, you approach the camp. Suddenly, you are stopped by three spears pointing straight at you.

Turn to page 92.

You open the closet door. A ball rolls out and hits you on the head. You step back onto a pair of skates and fall right on your bottom.

Finally the girl says, "It can't be in the closet. I never use it. I'm afraid to open the door."

You nod in understanding, and you know that you have no choice except to search the room bit by bit.

(continued on page 69)

You crawl along the floor, pushing and shoving junk out of the way. You scream when you kneel, with all your weight, on a triangular Lego. Then you continue lifting boxes, moving blocks, piling the clutter behind you as you crawl.

You shove aside the top of a Chutes and Ladders box and try to pick up a paper that is underneath it. But the paper is stuck to the floor.

"I spilled my juice there," the girl says.

You look at the paper and realize that it is the wrapping from the pig package.

The label on the paper says: Fayco Toys, 13 Gyp Street, Spiltmilk, Texas.

If you ask the girl to bring you the pig so that you can inspect it before you go to Texas, turn to page 93.

If you race from the room in order to catch the first plane to Texas, turn to page 94.

Afraid that he will become suspicious if you follow him, you decide to go home and try to figure out some other way to catch the man.

You know that the employee you suspect does business with your bank, because you have seen him there before. You decide to be at the bank when it opens in the morning.

At ten A.M. you are standing near a teller's window when the employee walks in. You stand casually near him, disguised so that he cannot recognize you. You watch as he makes a twenty-thousand-dollar deposit.

If you think that he is the culprit, turn to page 95.

If you think that he is not the culprit, turn to page 96.

If you think that there is more to this than meets the eye, turn to page 97.

Surrounded by children, you go into the school. Everything looks familiar to you, and suddenly you realize that this is the school you attended when you were in first and second grades. You are so surprised that, for a minute, you feel as though you are seven years old again.

Then you remember that you are a famous movie star being pursued by a kidnapper.

If you run down the corridor and into the art supply room, turn to page 98.

If you go into the kindergarten classroom, turn to page 100.

As the chauffeur moves toward you, you know you must think quickly or you will lose your advantage.

Suddenly, you have an idea.

You whisper your plan to the children, and they pretend not to notice the man who is walking toward them. Just as he reaches the excited circle of children, they scream and yell, waving their hands in the air and making silly faces.

The chauffeur is so surprised that he takes a step backward. That is when the girl standing behind him puts out her leg and trips the uniformed man.

Down he falls, and a horde of children swarms over him. Each of the man's arms is weighted down by three children; each leg has four children perched on it. The biggest kid in the school plops himself down on the chauffeur's chest, and the rest of the children surround him.

(continued on page 74)

You smile as you run into the school to call the police.

The second call you make is to the ice cream parlor down the street. Within an hour, three hundred and eighty-seven hot fudge sundaes are delivered to the school, one for every child.

The End

The water in the pool is crystal clear, and the fountain in the middle sprays out perfumed water. It is a hot summer night, and the pool looks so inviting that you cannot resist.

You dive right in. But when you come to the surface, you feel heavy and weighted down.

You realize, too late, that you are wearing all your clothes.

The End

You get to the banquet table and are awed by the choices of food laid out before you. Just then, the host of the party walks up to you.

"What can I get you to eat?" he asks genially. "May I recommend something?"

You do not want to offend this rich and powerful gentleman, so you nod your head yes.

"Which would you prefer?" he inquires as he points to the dishes and names them. You know that you must make a choice.

If you choose the escargot, *turn to page 101.*

If you choose tart tatin, *turn to page 102.*

If you choose cervelle de veau au beurre noir, *turn to page 103.*

You hold your fork in midair, turning your head slowly to see who is speaking. Three men are standing at the entrance to the dining room. The one in the middle is holding a pistol.

If you cooperate with the robbers, turn to page 104.

If you try to think of something you can do, turn to page 105.

You pretend that you are going to cooperate. Then, suddenly, you lunge for the rifle and grab it off the wall.

The man nearest you reaches out for your arm, but you swing the rifle around and hit the man right on the head. He falls, unconscious, to the floor.

"Don't move!" you say, brandishing the rifle in the direction of the other two men. "Now let's talk about who's in charge here."

The End

You nod to the men that you will cooperate. Slowly, you walk where they lead you. Then, suddenly, you break away and start to run.

I hope I can remember how to do it, you think, grateful that you once acted in a western and refused to have a stuntperson play the dangerous part.

You get to the rear of the horse and jump, using your arms as a lever to spring onto the animal's back. Without stopping, you grab the reins and kick the horse.

"Stop that person," you hear one man shout.

"Shoot the rat!" yells another.

"No! Then we won't get the ransom. Quick! Get in the car."

There is a road in front of you that runs between two cornfields.

If you gallop straight down the road, thinking that you have enough of a head start to make it to the highway, turn to page 106.

If you try to get the horse to jump over the fence that encloses the cornfield on the right, turn to page 108.

Two hours later, you open your eyes and find yourself tied to a chair, your arms behind your back.

"Our guest is coming around," says a strange voice.

"You'll never get away with this," you say.

"We already have," says the man. "All we need is for you to get on the telephone and call the studio. Tell them we have you, that you are safe. Then we'll talk to them about ransom."

The man dials and hands you the phone.

"Hello, Sammy?" you say to the head of the studio.

"How are you?" Sammy asks, his voice jolly.

"I'm safe," you reply.

"I'm glad."

"Well, I'm glad you're glad I'm safe, Sammy, but I have a problem."

"We all have problems," Sammy says.

"I know, Sammy. But this is a big one. I've been kidnapped, and they're holding me for ransom."

(continued on page 81)

"Well, get the heck out of there!" Sammy bellows.

"This is no joke," you say. "I need your help."

If you do exactly what your kidnappers say, and play it straight, turn to page 109.

If you try to transmit some sort of secret message, turn to page 110.

You feel yourself rising on the crest of the huge wave. Then you crash downward against the sandy bottom. To your relief, you discover that the water is shallow.

Exhausted, you crawl onto a wide, sandy beach. At the edge of the sand is the beginning of a tropical jungle.

If you crawl to the trees to get out of the sun, turn to page 111.

If you pull yourself clear of the water and cover your body with sand before going to sleep, turn to page 112.

You feel yourself tossed and shaken violently by the powerful surf. You are grateful that the rope is still secured to your wrist.

Then you feel yourself being lifted by a gigantic wave. When you come down, you are tangled in the lines. The raft is on top of you.

You try to release your wrist from the rope so that you can get to the surface for air. But you are tangled too tightly. There is nothing you can do.

The End

As you swim toward the raft, you catch sight of a shark's fin moving toward you. The shark has been attracted by the scent of blood from your wound.

You reach the boat and throw yourself inside. You can feel the shark pass under the raft. You remain still until the shark leaves. Then you clean and bind your wound.

You wait awhile, and then paddle close to shore before you step out of the raft and tow it to dry land.

You are trying to untangle the towline from the seaweed when you see a clear, jellylike blob, about the size of a small balloon, only an inch away from your hand.

Turn to page 114.

You swim along the shore, thinking it is more important to reach the land than it is to take care of your wound. Blood flows into the water from your cut.

(continued on page 86)

You do not see the fins of the sharks who have been attracted to you by the scent of blood. When you finally do notice them, it is too late.

The End

You struggle, thinking that if you can just grab hold of the rock it will stabilize you and prevent you from being sucked down into the sand. But the more you struggle, the quicker you sink.

Finally, you know that you are doomed. Your only consolation is that you will always be remembered for your lasting contributions to world geography.

The End

You flatten your body, distributing your weight evenly over the surface of the quicksand. And then you inch your way forward on the top of the sand, as if you are swimming on Jello.

Just as you reach out and grab hold of a branch, you hear voices.

Looking up in wonder, you see a rescue party heading in your direction.

"We found you!" they cry. "Our ship picked up the emergency directional signal on your life raft, and we followed it to this island."

You smile gratefully when they recognize who you are. There are advantages to being on the cover of *Time* magazine, you think.

The End

You start to climb. Still, you hear Mark and his people behind you.

Ahead, you see a small ravine covered with some skimpy bushes.

If you hide in the ravine, hoping that they will pass you by, turn to page 115.

If you try to make it to the top and across to the other side without stopping, turn to page 116.

You start around the base of the volcano. As you run, the noise of your pursuers grows fainter. Finally, you know that you have eluded them.

But just when you think you are safe, you nearly collide with an enormous grizzly bear, raised up on its huge hind legs.

Turn to page 117.

"Halt!" says a woman. "Who are you?"

"I know this person," says a man standing next to her. "This is a world-renowned explorer." You smile to yourself, grateful that your fame has identified you.

After you explain the purpose of your mission, you are escorted into the camp. You talk to Karen, all the time wondering if you really do wish to remain forever on the island with Mark's group.

If you return to Mark's group with Karen so that she can use her medical skills on the sick person, turn to page 118.

If you choose to stay with this group and let Karen go by herself, turn to page 119.

After looking at the pig, you leave for Texas.

There is only one commercial building in Spiltmilk, Texas: the Fayco Toy factory. You enter the building and ask to talk to the manager.

"May I ask who you are?" a woman inquires.

"I represent SLOP, the Society for Lovers of Pigs," you answer.

"Of course," she replies, trying not to giggle.

"I want to inspect your pigs," you tell her.

"I'll take you to our pig department," she says.

You walk alongside a conveyor belt so filled with animals that it looks as though it must lead to Noah's Ark.

The man in the pig department does not find SLOP very amusing.

"You're not from SLOP," he says to you. "There is no such thing. As a matter of fact, I know exactly who you are. I make it my business to know what the famous detectives in this country look like."

If you think you had better tell the man the truth about why you are here, turn to page 120.

If you try to talk your way out of this, turn to page 122.

You race down the stairs, taking two steps at a time. When you are halfway down, your foot lands directly on some forgotten marbles, and you fly the rest of the way to the bottom.

When you wake up you are in the hospital, your head swathed in bandages.

The first question you ask is, "When can I leave?"

"Sometime next week," the doctor answers. "You have sustained a serious concussion."

Sadly, you telephone Agent 337 and explain what has happened. "I'm sorry," he says. "We'll have to assign someone else to the case. We can't afford to lose the time while you recover from a careless accident."

The End

You have not solved the case. Make a different choice.

Return to page 70.

You may have thought that he could not be the culprit, because he only deposited twenty thousand dollars instead of the sixty thousand you gave him.

It is highly unlikely that an innocent employee in a store would make a twenty-thousand-dollar deposit all at one time.

Return to page 70 and make a different choice.

You go to your friend and tell him that it is your sad duty to report that all three of his employees are thieves.

"But how do you know that?" he asks.

"Because this morning the man deposited twenty thousand dollars. Since I paid sixty thousand for the coin, it is obvious that the money was split three ways.

"Brilliant," says your friend. "No wonder you are famous and rich."

The End

There is no one in the art supply room when you enter, but the shelves are filled with art materials. You wrap yourself in a flowered fabric, tie a circle of tissue-paper flowers around your head and walk out, carrying a huge pile of construction paper to hide your face.

(continued on page 99)

The kidnapper passes you by in the hall. When he is out of sight, you dash into the principal's office and call the police. They arrive while the kidnapper is searching the auditorium.

Congratulations. You have outwitted your captor.

The End

You dash into the kindergarten classroom and whisper to the teacher, "You've got to help me. I'm being pursued by a kidnapper."

The teacher gasps when she recognizes you. "Of course," she says. "Class, we're going to play a new game," she announces. She tells you to lie down on the floor and scrunch up into a ball. As the class makes a circle around you, the teacher covers you with a blanket.

Then she writes a note telling the school secretary to call the police. "Jennifer, please take this to the secretary in the office," she says to a little girl.

As Jennifer opens the door, the phony chauffeur walks in, looks around and walks out. The teacher smiles proudly, but you do not even know that you have been saved because you are under the blanket. Twenty-five little people are dancing around you, singing, "The cheese stands alone. The cheese stands alone. Hi Ho the Dairy-o, the cheese stands alone."

The End

You poke the small meaty piece of *escargot* with your tiny fork, and then you eat it.

"Umm," you say as you eat another hunk of the garlicky meat. "That's delicious. What is it?"

"Snails in garlic, parsley and butter," the host explains with a smile.

Now that you are chewing the snail, it's up to you to decide whether this is a good or a bad ending.

The End

You take a bite of *tart tatin*. You can taste the apple and the wonderful buttery, flaky crust. You decide that you have made a wise choice.

The End

If you are still hungry, you may return to page 76 and make another choice.

You take a forkful of the *cervelle de veau au beurre noir*.

You love it. The sauce is so tasty, and the meat so tender.

"What is it?" you ask.

"Calves' brains in a burnt butter sauce," he answers happily.

You have a hard time swallowing. The taste is great, but you are not sure if you like eating brains.

You decide whether this is a good or a bad ending.

The End

You decide that it is safer to do exactly what the robbers say. You watch as they go to each person in the room, collecting jewels. Some of the people are angry; others are crying. They all look helpless.

When the robbers get to you, the man with the pistol stands at your side. One of the other men reaches down to take your watch. It is your favorite. Each number is made of diamonds, and it was given to you after you completed your first picture.

You are so angry that you lose your good sense. You take the plate with the lobster mousse and shove it into the man's face. Immediately, his partner grabs you and hits you over the head.

The next thing you know, two paramedics are standing over you.

"Are they gone?" you ask, your head feeling as though it has been blown up to the size of a huge watermelon.

"Yes," says a paramedic. "But one of the guests recognized the thieves. The police say it won't be long before they are caught."

The End

You grip your chest and cry out in pain. Everyone in the room turns toward you as you fall to the floor, groaning in agony. A woman standing next to you bends down to help, and the others in the room move in your direction.

But there is one exception. One of the guests, who happens to be a close friend of yours, picks up a bottle of champagne. With one swift move, he hits the robber who is holding the pistol. Then several guests tackle the other two thieves and pin them to the ground.

"Are you all right?" your friend asks you.

"I'm terrific," you answer with a grin as you stand up. Several of the people in the room gasp in surprise. "I thought you might remember that old routine we used to practice in acting school," you say to your friend with a wink.

"You should get an Academy Award for that heart attack," your friend says to you.

The End

You kick the horse and lean forward, your head close to the horse's neck. You can feel the animal's powerful legs working hard beneath your body as she gallops at full speed down the hard dirt road.

You hear the hum of a car engine behind you. Suddenly, you feel the dust spray onto your face as the car passes you. The horse, startled by the car, rears on her hind legs. You feel yourself slipping off her back. You try to hold on, but there is no saddle, and you slide off the horse's back onto the road.

(continued on page 107)

Before you know it, you are surrounded by three angry men whose guns are pointing directly at you.

"We'll make certain that you won't have a second chance to escape," says the largest man.

The End

You do not think about anything except getting over the fence. You hope that the horse is capable of the jump.

Leaning close to the horse's neck, you grab her mane, pulling the reins to the right.

Without hesitating, the horse runs toward the fence and, with a coiling of her powerful legs, she jumps over.

You do not look back, but you can hear the car crash through the fence and continue into the field in pursuit of you.

Then you hear a whirring sound as the car's wheels spin in the soft dirt.

When you reach the other side of the field, you look back. You see the men trying desperately to push the car out of the deep ruts it has carved in the soft dirt.

Ahead of you, a dirt road intersects another field.

If you turn down the road toward the highway, turn to page 123.

If you cross the road, taking the horse over another fence and into the next field, turn to page 124.

"Come on, I know you," Sammy teases. "And you know what? I'm getting tired of all your jokes. Last time it was a telegram telling me you were quitting the picture right in the middle. Enough jokes. I've got to take a meeting."

"Sammy!" you yell desperately into the phone. "I'm not kidding this time!"

"Ever hear about the kid who cried wolf?" Sammy says. And then he hangs up.

The kidnapper turns to you. "He don't believe you, huh?" The man smiles with an ugly grimace. "Well, that's something we didn't figure on. Nothing we can do now except dispose of the evidence while there's still time."

The End

Since you were not blindfolded during the drive, you watched where you were going. You know that you are near the farmhouse where you filmed your first movie. Sammy's friend, Marty, was the director on that movie.

"Is Marty with you?" you ask.

"Yeah," says Sammy.

"Tell him I've been kidnapped and put him on the phone."

"Hey, what's happening?" says Marty when he gets on.

"Marty, I'm in trouble. I need your help. We've been friends for a long time, Marty. Ever since *Stranger in the Dust.*"

"Yeah, I know. You think I don't remember?"

"Wait a minute, Marty. I can't hear you. There's a plane flying overhead."

The kidnapper becomes suspicious and grabs the phone. "Just get a million dollars. I'll call you later."

After he hangs up, the man hands you a plate with a hot dog and potato chips on it.

If you eat, turn to page 126.

If you refuse to eat, turn to page 127.

You begin to make your way across the wide beach. Your mouth feels dry, and your lips are beginning to crack. You know that if you do not find fresh water to drink very soon, you will become too dehydrated to continue.

You finally reach the trees.

Suddenly, you hear a rustling of leaves and the unmistakable sound of someone or something walking.

If you hide behind the bushes to discover the source of the sounds, turn to page 128.

If you call, "Who's there?" hoping it is another person, turn to page 129.

You awaken when the sun is high overhead. You feel refreshed from your nap, but you are thirsty and know that you must find fresh water if you are to survive.

You make your way to the trees at the other side of the beach. Then you stop and listen carefully to the sounds of the jungle.

(continued on page 113)

Your heart leaps with joy when you hear the faint sound of a waterfall. When you reach the water, you see that it is clear and fresh. You smile, knowing that with the water and your knowledge of edible plants, you will be able to sustain yourself until a rescue party finds you. You know that they are probably looking already.

There are advantages to being famous and rich.

The End

You realize that this is the infamous sea wasp, a jellyfish that floats on top of South Pacific waters. Its venom is so powerful that if you are stung you will die within thirty seconds. You pull your hand away just in time.

You tow the raft onto the beach, far away from the bull sea lion.

You are sad to have lost all your exploring equipment when the plane went down. But you resolve to do your best in spite of the loss. After all, ingenuity is part of being a truly fine explorer.

The End

If you decide that you really don't like the dangerous life of an explorer and would rather be a movie star, turn to page 7.

You jump into the ravine and arrange the bushes so that they cover you. And then you wait.

You hear your pursuers desperately looking for you. You remain perfectly still.

Just as they are upon you, you glance down. Two feet away from you is a huge snake.

If you decide to stay perfectly still, turn to page 130.

If you would rather risk getting caught than remaining next to the snake, turn to page 131.

You continue to climb, even though you are breathing hard and your heart is beating triple time.

The noise of your pursuers grows faint, and you are thankful that you're in peak physical condition.

Just as you reach the top of the mountain, you hear a low rumble as if a freight train were passing by.

Holy cow! you think. *It's an earthquake!*

If you remain where you are, turn to page 133.

If you make a run for clear ground, turn to page 134.

The bear is angry. Just behind it are two playful cubs, and you realize that this is a female protecting her young. There is nothing more dangerous in all the world.

You try to back away, but the bear lunges for you. With one swipe of her powerful claw, she rips into your back.

In pain, you run until finally the bear gives up and returns to her cubs.

Exhausted, you crawl under some bushes and fall asleep.

When you awaken, there is a man standing next to you.

"Medical aid is on the way," he says.

"Are you a member of Mark's group?" you ask.

"No. Our leader is Karen," the man says. "She is a doctor. Lie still now and soon you will be safe. And sooner or later, we will be rescued."

The End

You return to Mark's group with Karen, proud to be taking part in the saving of a life. During the journey, you consider the opposing positions of the two groups. You have sympathy for both. But you truly believe that it is wicked of one group of people to dictate to another.

You do not know how long it will take, but you resolve that, for the remainder of your time on this island, you will devote yourself to the cause of *all* the inhabitants. If you employ wisdom and understanding, you are sure that you will be able to bring these two enemies together.

The End

Suddenly, you are overwhelmed by your need to see your home again. You know that you cannot remain on this island.

You explain this to Karen.

"I understand," she says. "Our desire to return home is rooted in our love for our families and friends. Even though they probably think we are dead, we have wives and husbands, parents and children who need us. We tried to explain this to Mark. We told him that we understand his position, that we, too, love the simplicity of life on this island. But it is a dream, one which we cherish and one which we know must come to an end. We cannot reject the real world. Those people we love are too important.

"Stay with us. You are welcome. We know that if we do not give up, someday we will be rescued."

The End

"If you have nothing to hide, you have nothing to fear," you tell the man. "Just show me your pigs and then we'll discuss identities."

"Hogs or sows?" the man asks.

"Hogs," you reply. "The ugly black ones with the white spots." *Just like the little girl's,* you think.

(continued on page 121)

The man gasps. "Why do you want to see those?"

"Because a little girl I know received a very special one in the mail recently."

"So that's where it went," the man says. "Wait till I get ahold of that kid who fills the orders."

"I'm afraid you'll have to wait a long, long time," you reply, pleased that you will have good news to report to Agent 337.

The End

"I'm not a detective," you say.

"You can't pull the wool over my eyes," the man says.

"I know," you say. "You only do that in the lamb department."

"Not funny," the man says as he pulls out a gun from his shoulder holster and points it straight at you.

The End

You turn down the road, unwilling to risk another jump. Urging the horse forward, you gallop at full speed toward the highway ahead.

When you reach the highway, you cannot see any cars. Sitting on your horse, you wait.

Finally a green pickup truck moves toward you. You jump from the horse onto the highway, flagging down the truck.

It stops, and you open the door and jump inside.

"Welcome," says the kidnapper, pointing a gun directly at you. "Too bad you didn't consider the fact that we might have something else to drive besides a limousine."

The End

"Just one more jump," you tell the horse, and she flies over the fence.

You gallop across the field, racing into the woods beyond. You do not know where you are, but you want to make certain that the kidnappers will not find you.

You ride through the trees for several hours, until you see a small farmhouse in the distance. You ride up to the house, dismount and knock on the door. The woman who answers cannot believe her eyes.

(continued on page 125)

You explain that you are in danger, and she immediately telephones the police. Then she makes you a cup of tea.

"I hope my children arrive home from school before the police come," she says. "If they don't see you, they'll never believe that the most famous movie star in the world was in our house."

"I'll tell you what," you say with a smile. "Bring them to the movie set next week as my guests."

The woman is thrilled, and you are grateful that you can do something special for the person who has saved your life.

The End

You begin to eat the food. Before you have finished, you feel yourself growing drowsy. *They drugged my food*, you think too late.

"Our movie star is nodding off," you hear a faint voice say. "Let's get out of here. This smart aleck may have sent that Sammy person a message in all that crazy talk. If we change to the mountain cabin now, they'll never find us."

You feel yourself being lifted. You struggle, but you are helpless to do anything.

The End

"I don't eat junk food," you say, thinking of all the chemicals in the meal. You don't mention that you suspect there might be knock-out drops in the mustard. Instead of eating, you close your eyes and fall asleep.

You are awakened when three men with guns crash through the door.

"Don't move!" yells one of the rescuers. The kidnappers freeze.

"How did you know we were here?" asks the phony chauffeur.

"This smart movie star talked to Marty about *Stranger in the Dust*. It was filmed right near here. Then our friend said something about a plane flying overhead. This is isolated farmland. Not many planes fly over this part of the country. When Marty said there was a plane flying overhead, it was exactly three-thirty, so we checked all the airport flight plans. There was only one plane flying around here at that time. We got out the slide rule and figured out where the plane would have been at exactly that time. And here we are."

You smile, grateful that you have a good mind. *Famous and rich is nothing compared to that,* you think.

The End

You hide, trembling with anticipation and fear. Finally, you grow impatient and stand up, exposing yourself to the sight of whatever is making the noise.

You know that on a volcanic island as isolated as this one, there are probably no dangerous animals. Whatever creatures were able to reach this place either swam or flew.

You look in the direction from which the noises came, and you are appalled to see a huge tiger rushing toward you.

Never make assumptions about unknown places, you think. That is the last thought you have.

The End

"Who's there?" you ask, your voice trembling with a combination of hope and fear.

You stand up and are amazed to see a man and a woman.

Before you can utter another word, they grab you and take you to their leader.

Turn to page 43.

Your heart is pounding. Out of the corner of your eye you see the snake rise from its coiled position. A huge hood opens at the back of its neck, and you know that this is a member of the cobra family, one of the most deadly snakes in the world. You want to scream in fear.

If you think you can stay still until the pursuers pass, turn to page 135.

If you think the cobra is ready to strike and you want to get out of there, turn to page 136.

You tense the muscles in your legs and leap from the ravine. Unfortunately, your pursuers are waiting for you.

In no time they catch you and bind you with ropes made of hemp.

Oh well, you think, *being a prisoner is better than dying from a snake bite.*

The End

You remain where you are. As the earth trembles, you watch the ground ahead of you break off and tumble into the lava-filled crater of the volcano.

Rocks slide down the mountain, dislodging other rocks. Soon, you, too, are rolling down the slope.

When the quake is over, you have escaped with only a few bumps and scrapes.

You are certain now that you will be found, for you know that seismic recording stations all over the world have recorded this quake. Soon teams of scientists will come to do research on the island. And you, along with all the others, will be rescued.

The End

Knowing that the quake could cause trees and rocks to topple over you, you make a run for the clear ground ahead.

Suddenly there is a huge jolt, and you feel the ground crumble beneath your body as you begin to slide.

When the earth stops shaking, you find that you have rolled halfway down the mountain. Your body is cut and bruised, but you are safe. You feel very lucky to be alive.

The End

You do not move. The pursuers are directly in front of you now, but they do not see you. The noise that they make frightens the viper. You watch as it slowly lowers its head and slithers away.

You wait until you are certain Mark's group is gone. Then you creep out of the ravine.

Now that you have eluded your enemy, you know that you can make it over the top of the mountain where you will find the other group. You feel sure that eventually you will all be rescued.

The End

You dive through the bushes with a scream. Your pursuers are right there, but you think that anything is better than being bitten by a snake.

But it is too late. Your movement has scared the snake. You feel a sharp sting in your leg.

The End